W9-BGO-638

Seriously, You Have to Eat

by Adam Mansbach

illustrated by Owen Brozman

Published by Akashic Books
Words ©2015 Adam Mansbach
Illustrations ©2015 Owen Brozman

ISBN: 978-1-61775-408-1
Library of Congress Control Number: 2015934081
First printing
Printed in Malaysia

Twitter: @AkashicBooks
Facebook: AkashicBooks
info@akashicbooks.com
www.akashicbooks.com

Adam Mansbach's books include two beloved, bad-word-filled "children's" books our publisher won't let us name here, as well as the real children's book *Seriously, Just Go to Sleep.* He is the author of the novels *Rage Is Back, Angry Black White Boy, The Dead Run,* and *The End of the Jews,* winner of the California Book Award. He has written for the *New Yorker,* the *New York Times, Esquire,* the *Believer,* and National Public Radio's *All Things Considered.* His daughter Vivien is seven.

www.AdamMansbach.com

Owen Brozman has illustrated for *National Geographic, Time Out New York,* Scholastic, Ninja Tune, Definitive Jux, and numerous other clients. He and Mansbach's previous collaborations include one of the aforementioned unmentionable books and the acclaimed graphic novel *Nature of the Beast.* His work has been recognized by the Society of Illustrators of Los Angeles, *Creative Quarterly* journal, *3x3* magazine, and elsewhere. He lives in Brooklyn, New York, with his wife and daughter, whose favorite food is bananas.

www.OwenBrozman.com

to all the kids . . . stay hungry

The sunrise is golden and lovely,
The birds chirp and twitter and tweet,
You woke me and asked for some breakfast,
So why in the world won't you eat?

The bunnies are munching on carrots,
The lambs nibble grasses and bleat.
I know you're too hungry to reason with but
Seriously, you just have to eat.

Your cute little tummy is rumbling
And pancakes are your favorite treat.
I'm kind of surprised that you suddenly hate them.
That's ridiculous, kid. Just eat.

The giraffes pluck the tender young leaves up,
The mice snack on seeds and on wheat.
No, sweetheart, I can't make spaghetti,
The meal has been served, honey. Eat.

If we were both pandas I'd know what to feed you,
But seafood is dicey, we're leery of meat.
Half the food at the market is really quite scary,
But guess what? You still have to eat.

You're not finished, and no, you can't go to school
In pajamas, a hat, and bare feet.
Whatever, put shoes on and bring me your plate,
My whole diet's the stuff you won't eat.

The sloth and the lemur, the chipmunk and cheetah,
The slow and the sleek and the fleet
Share one thing, my love: they make less of a mess
Than you when they sit down to eat.

How was school, hon? Hey, your lunch box is full.
How are you not passed out in the street?
How is it you're smart? How the heck are you growing
When you basically don't ever eat?

You know who loves dinner? The duck-billed platypus.
But I know I'm facing defeat.
This conversation is like a terrible song
That just plays and plays on repeat.

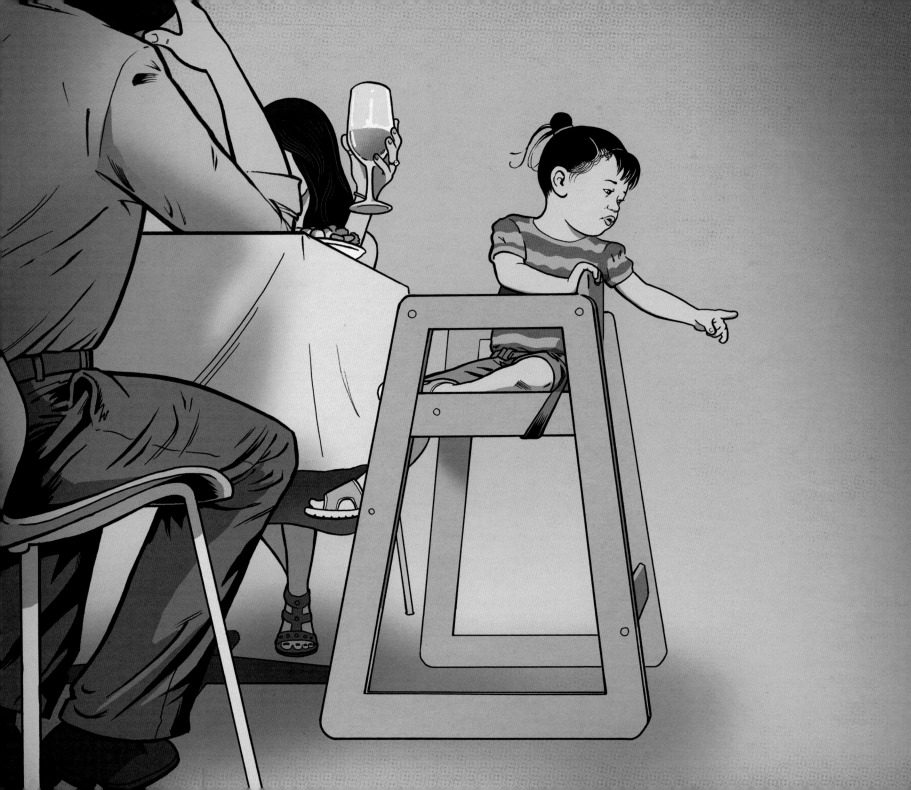

I hope you know it's really special
To go to a restau— Hey, back in your seat.
You kidding? This whole menu's gross to you
But a roll on the floor—*that* you'll eat?

Yum, this looks great. Five big bites, my darling.
Fine. Three, but don't try to cheat.
A lot of kids don't get asparagus,
Show a little respect for them. Eat.

Oh, now you're hungry? Tough luck, kitchen's closed.
Have some warm milk. For me a drink that smells like peat.
Pancakes? Yeah, right. It's bedtime, child,
It's way, way too late now to eat.

Fine. One pancake and that's it,
You're exhausting and I'm super beat.
And tomorrow we've got to rise early as roosters
To fight more about what to eat.

The End

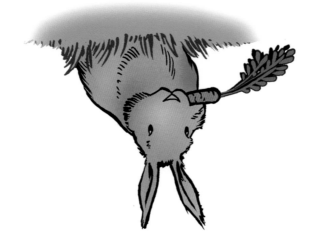

I'm pretty sure that you're malnourished
And scurvied. My failure's complete.
But on the bright side, maybe this is the night
You seriously just go to sleep.